This book belongs to ...

....

Tips for Talking and Reading Together

Stories are an enjoyable and reassuring way of introducing children to new experiences.

Before you read the story:

- Talk about the title and the picture on the cover. Ask your child what they think the story might be about.
- Talk about the times when you have travelled on a train and what it was like. Talk about your nearest train station.

Read the story with your child. After you have read the story:

- Discuss the Talk About ideas on page 27.
- Talk about how to catch a train on pages 28–29.
- Do the fun activity on page 30.

Have fun!

Find the Eiffel Tower hidden in every picture.

For more hints and tips on helping your child become a successful and enthusiastic reader look at our website **www.oxfordowl.co.uk.**

Going on a Train

Written by Roderick Hunt and Annemarie Young
Illustrated by Nick Schon, based on the orginal
characters created by Alex Brychta

OXFORD
UNIVERSITY PRESS

The children were excited. They were going to France on a train. Gran was taking them to EuroParc near Paris.

Kipper was a bit worried.

"Everyone speaks French in France," he thought. "I can't speak French."

First they had to catch a train to London. Mum and Dad were going with them to see them off at St Pancras Station.

The train arrived and Dad said, "Press that button when it lights up. It will open the doors. Then we'll find a seat."

In London, they went down a long escalator to an Underground station.

"We're going down to the Tube train now," said Gran.

"Look," said Gran. "There's the roller-coaster at EuroParc."

"It looks scary," said Kipper.

The train came and they got on.

They soon arrived at St Pancras International Station.
"Look at that roof!" said Biff. "It's huge."

"It's time to say goodbye," said Mum. "You must check in and find your seat on the Eurostar."

"Enjoy yourselves," said Dad.

"Wow!" said Kipper. "Is this our train?"

"Yes," said Gran. "Our seats are in carriage 10."

Gran put her case in the luggage bay.

"Let's look for our seats," said Chip.

They found their seats, but a man and a little girl were sitting in them.

"I think these seats are ours," said Gran.

"Pardon!" said the man. He was French. "I am sorry,"
he said. "Our seats must be on the other side of the aisle.
We must move, Emily."

The man smiled at the children. "Is your grandmother taking you to EuroParc?" he asked.

"How did you guess?" asked Biff.

"Ah!" laughed the man. "I live nearby. Emily likes to stay with me, so she can visit EuroParc every day."

"Can Emily sit with us, please?" asked Biff.

"Then she can teach us to speak French!"
said Kipper.

Emily sat with the children and Monsieur Simon
sat with Gran. The train began to move out of the
station.

The train picked up speed very quickly. Soon it went into the tunnel under the English Channel.

"My ears went pop," said Kipper.

"Bonjour is hello in French," said Emily. "But
don't worry. Everyone speaks English at EuroParc."

"Pardon?" said Kipper.

In Paris they caught a special train called The EuroParc Express.

"This is the fourth train we've been on today," said Chip.

The next day they met Emily and her grandfather at EuroParc.

"Bonjour," said Kipper.

"Bonjour!" said Emily.

"I'd like a ride on that roller-coaster," said Gran.

"Who's coming?"

"Not me!" said Kipper. "I'll show you the ride I want to go on."

"What is it?" asked Gran.

"Not another train!" laughed Gran. "Aren't you tired of trains?"

"No way! I love trains," said Kipper.

Talk about the story

What word did Kipper learn to say in French?

Which train do you think Kipper liked best?

Why do people go on trains?

Where would you like to go on a train?

How to catch a train

1. Buy your ticket.

2. Check the display board to find the platform number.

3. Go and wait on the platform.

4. Wait for the train to stop.

5. Press the button to open the door.

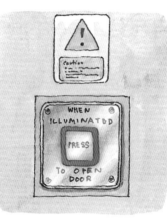

6. Find a seat.

7. Stay close to the grown ups you're with.

A maze

Help Kipper find the right train track to take him home to Little Ted.

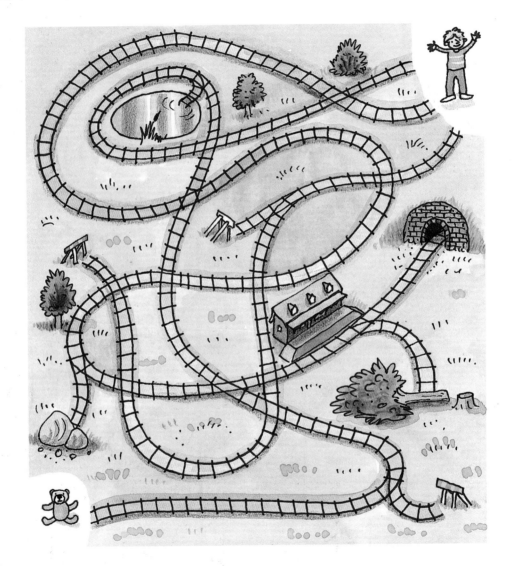

FIRST EXPERIENCES WITH Biff, Chip & Kipper

Have you read them all yet?

Kipper's First Pet

Learning to Swim

Going to the Dentist

Going to the Hairdresser

Going to the Doctor

Going on a Plane

Let's Recycle!

Fun at the Farm

Kipper Gets Nits

Starting School

A New Baby

FIRST EXPERIENCES Flashcards 55 cards

Also available:
- At the Hospital
- At the Optician
- At the Vet
- At the Match
- At the Dance Class

Read with Biff, Chip and Kipper
The UK's best-selling home reading series

Phonics   First Stories

Level 1
Getting ready to read

Level 2
Starting to read

Level 3
Becoming a reader

Level 4
Developing as a reader

Level 5
Building confidence in reading

Level 6
Reading with confidence

Phonics stories help children practise their sounds and letters, as they learn to do in school.

First Stories have been specially written to provide practice in reading everyday language.

OXFORD
UNIVERSITY PRESS

Great Clarendon Street, Oxford OX2 6DP
Text © Roderick Hunt and Annemarie Young 2009
Illustrations © Nick Schon and Alex Brychta 2009
First published 2009
This edition published 2013

10 9 8 7 6 5 4 3 2 1
Series Editors: Kate Ruttle, Annemarie Young
British Library Cataloguing in Publication Data available
ISBN: 978-0-19-273514-0
Printed in China by Imago
The characters in this work are the original creation of Roderick Hunt and Alex Brychta who retain copyright in the characters.